Samuel L. Clarke

Divine Revelation on the Lamb's Book of Life

Samuel L. Clarke

Divine Revelation on the Lamb's Book of Life

ISBN/EAN: 9783337780388

Printed in Europe, USA, Canada, Australia, Japan

Cover: Foto ©Andreas Hilbeck / pixelio.de

More available books at **www.hansebooks.com**

Divine Revelation

ON THE

LAMB'S BOOK OF LIFE

BY SAMUEL L. CLARKE

BOSTON, MASS.:
PUBLISHED BY SAMUEL L. CLARKE
1895

INTRODUCTORY.

THE LAMB'S BOOK OF LIFE is written to introduce simply the coming of divine truth in every degree of life, and to uncover that which has been so long concealed from the world. This revelation is meant to interpret and place in its proper state the language of God, so as to instruct correctly the unlearned in spirit in everything that is really necessary for man to know in order to live a godly life. This revelation has cut a world-wide channel through the world, wherein it has spread its great waters and opened in the immense channel a sure and safe passage to life immortal. The writings show and prove to the world, among those who have eyes to see and understanding to understand, that there is no other power used to accomplish the works of the perfect salvation than the progressive, destructive, and creative words of God, which exist in three immortal, infinite, and all-powerful forms,—Divine Word, Spirit, and Truth combined. There is no other power, tact, nor science used to fulfil the work declared to take place with the members of these truths than the three first elements of life which I named, although there are many more things connected therewith to complete the irresistible power, the full machinery, which constructs the three elements, which will be found in these writings.

This revelation does not mean to assert, nor to convey the understanding that the members of the perfect truths will be plunged very suddenly into incessant happiness by reading and receiving these writings, nor that they will be cast down to despair and death because they irrationally refuse to grasp it when they first hear of it. But it means to work its own way reasonably and graciously, and to find and prepare its own members the true breasts to lodge in, by the purity and straightness of its work, which must work gradually and surely wherever it finds a lodging-seat. It discourses herein, and in the complete book of "Divine Psychology," that the world has undoubtedly a new epoch of divine righteousness, which has caused a great breach in the world, and the turmoiling of nations, where the purity of the old and the new eras shall combine, and weed out all formality and impurity that conflict with the true life.

The combining of the old and new truths has weeded out the terrible reign of sin from those hearts who took hold of the perfection of truth when it first and suddenly appeared in the world; and it shall continue to renounce the dead and useless works perpetrated by the so-called children of light, who shall take hold of these truths hereafter; and the same shall lay hands on their spirits and nature, so that those who labor for the advancement of the perfect right may see and behold the realities there are in the era of purity, light, and understanding of all the true principles prepared for mankind to inherit.

THE LAMB'S BOOK OF LIFE.

PART I.

[See Circular, showing the power and present mission of these writings. See " Divine Psychology," on the fulfilment of prophecies, God's impartial judgments against sin in humanity, and the " Book of Seven Seals," opened to the world, showing how mankind is to be reclaimed.]

THIS revelation, which is the late precept of divine truth, is sent, a direct message from God, to the world to issue among those who are growing very weary, and whose hearts are failing them, and who are hopeless because of the long period of time that God saw fit to withdraw his face and power from the world, and gave the world up to be servants of sin and uncleanness according to their desires. Many have suffered severely and endured everything which was allowed to come against them to try and purge every motive, taste, love, and desire in man. All the moral world has suffered to come to the end of the terrible reign of sin ; and they must continue to endure while waiting for those blessed promises, that long-sought-for glory, rest, and perfect satisfaction, and the fulness of the power of Christ to be demonstrated to the world, and to attain that unchangeable power, unerring' faith, hope, love, and uninterrupted submission that will lay siege to the smallest particles of sin and uncleanness, so that one final offering for sin will be made once for all. The foundation upon which every one is to stand now and henceforth, to be worthy of, and to receive the price to purchase the living promises of Almighty God, which

are now concealed from the world by the realization of the union
of the first and second coming of Christ, is for the readers of
this revelation to hear, believe, and receive the one claim, which
is the broad basis upon which I stand supported by the unequal
power of God's wisdom and understanding to write of the perfect and imperfect life, and to issue it among the people, and
that is this : the blessed Lord and Saviour, Jesus Christ, which
is the pure word of God, has appeared the second time into the
wicked world to reclaim falling and suffering humanity; but he
does not exist in the world in a visible form of flesh and blood,
but in a new and refined, pure, doctrinal revelation. Christ is
not flesh and blood, bone and sinew, as he was when he prefig-
ured his spiritual body and power at his first coming into the
world.

It must be understood — and this is purely godly reasoning,
— that everything that has taken place, both small and great,
since mankind put on the mortal image, which is death and hell,
was God's concealed methods to work out the fulness of divine
righteousness, and the establishment of the immortal image, the
life of Christ. The many material changes which God has
caused to take place before and between the coming of the
fleshly and spiritual Christ, after using the flesh to prefigure
what is contained in the spiritual world, were merely to fulfil
what was determined against the devil's kingdom, which is set
up in the spirits and nature of men in its grandeur. Now the
same cleansing and healing powers are in the spiritual world,
and are ready for use whenever one feels that he is in need of
them, and has the price to procure them. The healing, cleansing, destructive, and creative powers which shall change the
vile souls of men among those who will hear, believe, and
receive Christ's coming to reign are in the pure words of God ;
and those spiritual saints who are sleeping in the material saints

shall, by receiving the pure word, awake and meet Christ at his coming to reign, by the power of his Father's omnipotent wisdom and understanding, over all sin and uncleanness.

My claim is hereby clearly understood. It is, Christ is now in the world among sinners and unclean men the second time ; but not as before, lest he build upon the old foundation and fail to make improvements, to take away the Cross, the strain, and the responsibilities. To them who are seeking him earnestly shall he appear, and be seen as he is, in this revelation, in language, spirit, and truth, which issued from the Almighty to fulfil and realize every promise which he has made unto the just since the world began, and to reward the unjust.

It is not for man to lean to his natural understanding and false reasoning to learn the real truths concerning what has taken place, for what purpose, what shall be hereafter, and why God should allow such things to be. Such questions are vain repetitions for the natural man, because God never has and never will make his determinations and mysteries fully known to the sinful man, whose desires and self-will are his own glory and intelligence. God has foreordained to give himself in full to the people who have obtained the price to purchase his life ; and there is no power to deprive the people of God of receiving his life when they reach the appointed time for the blessings to shower upon them. And for those who are fashioned with sinful tendencies, who will not receive the true Gospel of God, there is no such thing as escape from the wrath of God, for the day of escape is far spent.

This is to discover and locate the realities of the perfect world and the falsities of the imperfect world, and to reveal the workings of sin and righteousness in pure and plain language, just as the perfect and the imperfect are lettered, but slumbering, upon the pages of humanity. When this is done, I shall have proved, by the writings of the Holy Bible, that Christ, the Saviour of men, has already made his second appearing to the human world, and is working out men's eternal salvation in a concealed way.

Wherever Christ has appeared unto the human world the first time, in hope of the perfect salvation, he and his holy saints are slumbering in humanity, in wait for Christ's second appearing, which must be accomplished within the soul and nature of men, to quicken the slumbering substances, to give power to humanity to overcome every particle of the imperfect life, so as to receive the perfect whole.

This can, and shall, be done by receiving Christ's second coming to reign over his many enemies, which live and reign in men's customs, styles, laws, doctrines, wisdom, judgment, and understanding. The agreement in humanity between Christ's first and second appearing will form and establish the fulness of divine power in the soul, even as sin has come to the full in the souls of some people, to reject that which is eternal. But sin must reign in humanity until each person for himself receives the full life of Christ, both spiritually and physically, which must involve the teachings of his first and second coming combined.

The wisdom and the understanding of the natural world is one thing, and it belongs to the world; but the wisdom and understanding of God is entirely different, and conflicts with that of men.

To endure in the world and to do good unto men for the praise and glory of men is one thing, and such belongs to the kingdom of men; but to endure and to do good for the kingdom of heaven's sake, according to the true calling and purposes of God, is entirely different from that of men, and they disagree and conflict in their methods of work; for righteousness in the council of God is wickedness and crime in the sight of men in some instances, and righteousness in the council of men is wickedness and crime in the sight of God in many cases; although they of the world are allowed to use the name "Jehovah" the same as the elect, and to use the same language as though they were chosen by the power of the Almighty to do their unjust work.

To read the Bible, and to imagine that you are then summoned to work in the Lord's vineyard is not genuine; it is absolutely a false conception, which has gone into the world and has already taken hold upon thousands, and influenced them to make themselves ministers and teachers of Christ.

The Bible is the testimony of divine righteousness in the man of God, and the true guide to sustain him in every good work in life when the Holy Spirit quickens him to understand its teachings.

The Bible was not ordained and given for disputers, pickers, philosophers, and free-thinkers to chew upon, to strive in conversation for rivalry; but it is a medium of divine and physical righteousness, and a guide and teacher for every man who is godlily inclined in every vocation of life. And if each person of trade and profession dealt justly by his fellow men, the Holy Spirit would quicken each person to those parts of the Holy Scriptures best suited for his condition, without taking thought.

The true teachings and understanding of the Bible are not brought to the minds of men and made to rule over sin in them day by day, because they fail to regard and establish the true and honest way of living. And for this cause the power of the Word of God, which he has revealed. from heaven for men's salvation, is stamped under foot, and crushed out of existence simply because men hate the true, the honest, and straight way.

In order to be engaged in the service of Almighty God, he

must, according to his own purposes and determinations, call you away from your own will and desires, and choose you to be an instrument of his glory, just as men employ their servants to do certain work, and a certain amount of work, for so much salary. And no man on earth has entered the callings involved in the service of almighty power unless God revealed himself, instructed him plainly what he should do in order to live to God's glory, and what he should cease from doing in order to please God.

The idea of studying out and searching for the wisdom of God by the theory and philosophy of the world, the wisdom of men according to the prevailing custom of men in their science of divinity, is a fraud and illusion; and this is making men more and more depraved and opposed to true godliness. Man cannot possibly serve God to his glory simply because he can or would like to; neither can he enter the services of God because he feels that it is his duty to do something in that line because the Bible states that such is required of man. If men take this duty upon themselves, they evoke for themselves wrath and curses; and their reward is not of God, neither from God, but of men and from men, although they are laboring falsely in the name of God, and imitate the chosen seed.

There are thousands of people who claim falsely to be servants of Christ, and have erred and worse than deceived themselves on this very same point, by assuming the names of servants of Christ. They have made themselves teachers and servants to satisfy their own fleshly lust, which is the world in them making errors, by lusting to do in the name of godliness what they are not organized to do, just as it lusts in them after that which pertains unto the world visibly. And this is the scheme of sin to deceive them and lead them into snares of wickedness with a godly object in view, as it does with worldly objects in view.

A person can be covetous and vainglorious in striving to
attain to certain perfection of godliness according to men's
philosophy of godly perfection just as truly as he can be covetous and vainglorious in seeking the wealth of the world. It is
sin, I care not what course it pursues or what profession of life
it follows.

Many strive for wealth, glory, and the honor of men ; but
there are very few who obtain it to their souls' satisfaction,
because they are unable to reach all the principal resources that
swell the current of wealth, fame, and honor. And those who
do obtain the wealth of the world to their souls' pleasure are the
kings, queens, and princes of wealth, among whom it is reserved
and handed down to their heirs. The riches of God, which he
has foreordained to confer upon the heirs of salvation, are to
those who are the exact likeness of his image, both in substance
and spirit. It is not possible for one to receive the inheritance
of righteousness when he has not the purchase possession.
Divine righteousness was prepared in the beginning for all
mankind, and not for animal kind.

There are millions and millions of people like unto mankind
apparently, but in reality there are very few genuine human
beings in comparison with the various animals, reptiles, fowl,
and fishes which are existing in human forms. Unless people
are thoroughly tried by the pure laws and doctrines of life, it is
more than difficult to distinguish the human-statured animals
from the human race. Refinement, education, politeness, dex-
terity, and the schemes of business talents do not constitute,
really, a human being as God preordained him to be in his perfection. Still, time and rigid teachings and strict regard and
obedience to the principles of the perfect laws and doctrines
will cause the human-statured animals to progress from the
animal world, and to be transformed by fire into genuine human

beings, under which name they are now going and representing falsely.

Animal principles and appetites of various sorts, which bear rule over every mite of humanity, make them everything but genuine human beings. Years and years of training of animal dispositions have made the animal race more sagacious and prosperous in the world than the real human beings; because the world is their home, and they have no other glory and pleasure in life, and no other aim to achieve, than to go as far as the world will allow them.

The actual human beings cannot prosper while they look wholly to the glory of the world, as does the animal race, because they are warned that they have souls to give over to destruction, and souls immortal to gain, wherein satisfaction, peace, and pleasure reign, and that the world of vanity is not their home and glory. As long as this conscious and rational thought is continually rubbing and wearing down the desires, loves, and hopes in the world, there is no power of courage nor any energy to go forth with work of any worth and be successful, as the members of the world can do.

The involuntary doctrines taught by divine nature in the rational thoughts of the elect are continually condemning and imprecating the polluted glory and honor of the world until the King of eternal glory comes in and creates the true glory for all useful things. This is the reason why the true elect cannot prosper in the business world. They are drifting from place to place without success, awaiting the appearing of the heavenly glory, which is the primary basis of their prosperity, peace, and contentment. Man's final conclusion with the world, and exemption from its prevailing sins and curses, depend entirely upon his taste and desire to do right, and upon gods in the same before man entered into the world.

If a man has a ruling desire to live in the world in acquire-
ment of its glory and success, and never wishes for anything
different from that which the world contains, it is unwise for the
man whose life, glory, and success are in the divine world to
persuade the worldly man to seek the life beyond the world.
The worldly man can be taught the true way to live in the
world, which is his life and pleasure ; but never attempt to urge
upon him the doctrines of the other world. It produces mixtures
and non-success if true godliness is urged upon a person who
cannot possibly receive it to accomplish any good. The pure
life of Christianity should not be taught to persons who have
not that power of conscience and godly influence working
within them ; for if they are left at large to act, speak, and perform according to their own feelings as to which world they
shall turn their attention, time, talent, and skill for life and
success, their own conscience will compel them to choose the
life best suited for them to live and enjoy, because the power
must rule when they have heard and learned the chances which
they have in either world, and what they are required to be and
to do in order to have success. That which one is required to
do to achieve success in striving to obtain earthly glory is a
fatal curse if he is striving to attain the riches of the other
world. The striving to obtain earthly glory, honor, riches, and
blessings ceases as soon as the eternal progress of heavenly
glory sets in.

I care not what a man's talent or occupation may be, if he
has a secret thought working with zeal and hope to reach a
purer and more perfect knowledge of God, it will reveal itself
and find its heaven, just as wickedness will search out new plans
to accomplish its mission by manifesting itself in man.

Sin needs no persuasion, for it is already destined to perform
its work manifestly ; so will the righteousness of God work-

ing in man develop and find in itself peace and justification without persuasion, whatever befalls it or whatever condemnation is maliciously brought against it.

The life of God working in man is a secret trust, support, and safeguard for the man who lives the life of God, just as much as gold, silver, and riches are the secret trust, support, and comfort of man in the temporal world, and such as are conformed to the glory of the world. And it is impossible to live the pure life of God and be conformed to the customs of the world, and at the same time prosper in both worlds in your essential aims and desires.

The natural man is the substance of the world, and in the bowels of the earth ; and he must be taken from the world to work out, receive, and live the pure life of God to his own glory and honor, just as men choose the different substances of the temporal world for their glory and honor, and to use in any way that they may see fit. The election of man as heir to eternal happiness, the mansions of perfection, depends wholly upon two conditions : first, his desire and love for the life of God ; second, it depends upon God's predestinations of man's election to the throne of eternal life. No man can be chosen, nor made an heir to the throne of life unceasing, until he is required of God to perform a certain kind and portion of work according to his will. A man may be ever so zealous to turn from the glory of the world, and to enter into the holy services of almighty power to perform some work to his glory before the specified time — it will be of no effect in changing the predestinations of God, neither will it have effect until the arrival of the appointed time. And if such zealot were not ordained to enter into the services of God, that worldly and selfish zeal to be God's freeman is all in vain ; but if he is the chosen seed according to God's glory and honor, that continual zeal is preparing him for

the appointed time by making him more and more conformed
to divine will when the appointed time is fulfilled.

Yet all are to run and not falter, and wait in faith where it is
bestowed; for the election of man to the throne of the righteousness of God is sure, as he has promised it to all who contain
his substance, receive his Word, and partake of his Spirit as
pure as he bestows it. There is another great thought of man's
election to eternal happiness, and his final sentence to misery
and woe, and, lastly, death, which seems to some, or to many, to
be unjust of God,— to allow the suffering of humanity to prevail,
when he is the power that causes man to go into sin, that he may
learn the craft of sin, and at last know the agony of sin in every
degree of the mortal life.

Again, it seems unmerciful on the part of the Almighty to
allow such brutal suffrages to continue, while at the same time
he has power to cause them to cease, and to give peace and
satisfaction to his people, and to make them to know the true
and unerring way, his will and pleasure, and to avoid the many
errors that purchase the penalties of sin. But God will not
cause a thing to cease, whether it produces suffering or death,
while such is tending directly to the fulfilment of his predestinations; therefore, in this case, the power that is all-powerful
has no power to cause a thing to cease that is drifting on to the
true end, where the cessation of trouble will stand.

PART II.

THE complete book of "Divine Psychology" means that there is a new, pure, powerful, and more advanced truth in existence, which means the return of the original life to man. It means to destroy and purge out the impure life, which is death, and which, by degrees, stealthily crept into humanity and corrupted it. It does not mean to destroy any existing good nor welfare of man, but it means to cleanse all things that were made for man's glory and honor. When I say : To cleanse all things, it means to cleanse the motives, aims, desires, and loves of man, so that every man of truth will work for the welfare of his fellow creatures, and not for the mere accumulation of wealth.

This book shows how the author of it discovered and revealed the perfect doctrines of life ; and how the members who are connected with it conducted themselves, which caused the discovery of the new world, its laws and doctrines, and also the fallacies there are in the old world. And it also shows how the works and trials of the author concur with the writings of the Holy Bible, the words of which were the great waters for man to sail upon, in search of every sin and crime, and to discover the new world prepared for the saints of the living God. It shows that each marked change which took place while producing the writings contained in this book was deliberately ordained by the Holy God for righteous purposes ; and each significant change was a fiery fulfilment of the Holy Scriptures.

The complete book of "Divine Psychology" clears up every mystery that heretofore densely overshadowed the mission and purity of the perfect truths, and reached the extreme depths of sin and iniquity which underlay and overlay the complete whole of perfection in the forthcoming age. This book does not mean to exalt nor to honor beyond measure the material body of him whom God used as an instrument to perform and outline the complete whole of the perfect salvation. It means to give due honor and respect to everything that God has created and formed for his glory, whether it be man, beast, herbs, fowl, wealth, wisdom, style, or anything in existence working to this end; and there is nothing that exists that is not tending to this purpose and end in some way.

Shall God destroy that which he has created and caused to perform, when it is tending to promote good? Or shall he be indignant over his own creation, formation, and production?

The things that exist unto the destruction of almighty power, when the time arrives for them to be brought to naught, are destroyed by the power and wrath of God, and according to his glory, as much as though they were created and formed to his glory.

The wrath of God against the things fitted unto destruction is his method of destroying the agents ruled out of use after he has finished his purposes with each kind created unto destruction. The almighty power of divine nature, in its purposes, created and formed many machineries, weapons, and agents to use in the performance of God's work, that it may be carried out in perfect order, as man has been empowered and endued with wisdom to discover and patent the many agencies to accomplish their work in the temporal world.

After the more-advanced discoveries come into existence and use, they destroy, or lay aside, the old in honor of the new; so does the growth of immortality put down the mighty strains and unjust servitude,—the old and impure method of serving God, as it is called,—and establish a civil, free, and pure way of living the life of God.

What advantage is it to the man who disbelieves in and opposes the will, to become a servant of God? There is none. But if God ordained a man to carry out his purposes against the man's will and sentiments, the man is not to be rewarded, nor to become great in the sight of men; it is solely that God's determination in the creation and formation of that man may be fulfilled.

How long will it take a man to become fully conformed to the perfect will,—if it is determined that he shall,—if the man is opposed to the will of the Almighty? It depends upon what purposes God has to work out of that man's case, who is naturally opposed to his will. It may possibly take as long as it will take a child to learn the alphabet, and to read and write well, when he has no taste for learning. So can the opposing man's spiritual progress grow, by gradual degrees.

How can man ever learn the perfect will of God? By knowing and feeling what is the perfect will, and knowing, also, what he is to do in the different walks of life in order to please the Divine Spirit.

How shall man know the perfect will of God, when it works differently with each one who is chosen according to the will of the perfect life? After a man enters the blessed calling of the new life, he is to work, seek, and perform each day in harmony with his controlling desires, seeking that which he loves,—the perfect will of God.

When God has chosen you to accomplish some work and to do his pleasure in all you think, say, or do, he will not instil his desires into your heart against his own will and purposes. Consequently, there is no way to accomplish anything against the determinations of God when he has prepared you to do his will and good pleasure.

He is, then, the Creator and Ruler of your every desire and

pleasure, by which you are to gain access into his perfect will without fear or doubts, while you look to the ruling power of the mind and body. For this reason, there are no snares nor blessings to step into against the perfect will and pleasure of God, for all your steps are ordered according to God's will when you put on life eternal.

What is your idea concerning the present and future life, and concerning the different faiths and denominations, in regard to their all being the heirs to the same throne and kingdom ? Well, what are the ideas of the Bible, and what individual faith and denomination now in existence does it wholly support, condemning all others ? When this question is answered, and the mysteries that darken all denominations are cleared up, and the true denomination is created and brought forward and established, then it will be very easy to understand what created the many faiths, opinions, and denominations in honor of the present and future life, and why they have not heretofore combined in honor of the millions and millions of truths which prevail in part among them all.

If all the different faiths and denominations, with their entire truths, were brought together and combined according to the glory of the Almighty, and all the fallacies purged out, they would produce a complete whole,— the fulness of the life of pure godliness.

The Bible is the word of God,— messages directed from heaven to falling and rising humanity,— and before man can take the words of God, he must first believe and receive the writings of the Bible as true, whether he can interpret its meanings or not. All the different ideas concerning the present and future life, and all the different creeds, were taken from the Bible ; and each believer thinks, or pretends to believe, that his faith and manner of worship are true, or as near right as they can ever be in this world. He also thinks that all the rest of the faiths and opinions are false, and believers in them will not be received into heaven, that far-away home, until they deny their false faiths and join his.

Very well, then ; suppose you find a man who is sent from God to combine all denominations, faiths, doctrines, and opinions by a simple, small, family-like system, and to place each tenet in the proper state, where it will acquiesce, and by so doing will see the purposes of God in allowing the many faiths and denominations to come into existence, to prevail, and condemn the root from which they all sprung.

I say that the ideas of the Bible are my ideas ; and if the Bible is false, I am false ; and if the Bible is true, and was revealed from heaven to reclaim mankind, I am commissioned to do the same, by fulfilling the laws and doctrines of the Bible upon every one whom the power of the Almighty draws unto me according to his purposes, in honor of the fulness of his life, in the dispensation of the perfect doctrines and laws, to rule over man in righteousness. I have no ideas of my own, no theory, no understanding, no desire, no will.

The things that are within me, in whatever form or expression, are God's ; so, then, the motives and desires there are within me are God's, and they will obey his teachings, and walk in his way in all things ; and there are no errors in them, because they proceeded from him, and I manifest them as he infuses them into my heart.

I know that man cannot of himself become faultless and flawless, even if he sacrifices all that he owns or desires naturally, and also lays down his own life to become immortal. Of his own efforts, man is but mortal, and is no more than the man who would be opposed to such. Why so ? Because it is the man's own glory and strivings, and not the pleasure of God ;

and if such is the pleasure of man, thinking that he will attain a certain state of perfection, God will allow him to strive and do all he desires to do; for he will grant the desire of every living thing, as far as they have obtained force to carry it out, and such things can be used as ensamples and warnings for those who would pursue, and for those who would not pursue, the false way.

Man cannot, under any circumstances whatever, serve God until he can reason and think from God's being, and desire, love, receive, obey, and yield his body to obey God's will, as he was commended unto sin in the world.

Although dissimulation was the righteousness and curse of the old law, by which the law came, just so death came by the Cross and destroyed the false glory and honor unto God, that you may receive the perfect image of his Son, Christ, who is the pure and everlasting word of life, and makes you forgetful of the duties there are to those who are alive to the Cross of Jesus Christ. The Cross came not by the unrighteousness of this generation, nor was it destroyed by the righteousness of this generation; but according as it was ordained, so is it in the workings of righteousness in all things.

What code of laws and doctrines has God prepared to bring men to perfect repentance and to confer upon them eternal salvation? Are men to go blindly along the paths of salvation unaware of what shall be their fate, not knowing what course to pursue, or what they are to perform, or how to act in order to be pure in the sight of the perfect truths?

When you receive the Spirit of the perfect life, you receive the pure laws and doctrines, and the perfect will of God, in that Spirit which will not lead and teach you in all ways just as it is leading another who is partaking of the same life; because the condition and needs of each one who is subject to the will of the

Almighty are different, hence the leadings and teachings must issue to each one to suit his condition.

There are no other written methods nor codes of law and doctrine for man to learn consciously in everything he does, in order to be fashioned to the glory of the immortal life, than that there is a certain way to eat, drink, and enjoy life, in order to acquire an education, wealth, and the honor of men. Then, if a man should feel that he would like to connect himself with the immortal doctrines and their methods of teaching and leading, and live in honor of the immortal life, what would be the first step he would be required to make in order to be successful in receiving the higher truths ? What method of conditions have you to offer to save men from the sins and crimes of the world ? If a man's controlling desire, trust, hope, and affection should become absorbed into the life of the perfect truths, he would not be refused the full teaching of the pure way to life ; but such teachings would be in harmony with his condition, and also with the conditions of those with whom he is associated in life, so that no acts of injustice should be done to them. And in all cases, those with whom he is connected in life shall have all necessary advantages to empower them to see the purity and straightness of the immortal doctrine's will in doing work of this kind, whether they desire to see it, or would not see it right after doing all that can be done ; for the wickedness and blindness of an opponent shall not compel the holy doctrines to deal unjustly, to retaliate, as the world does, in case of opposition.

The matter of leaving off old associates, and the discontinuation of receiving the established method of teaching the divine doctrines in a material sense, would be of no progressive importance to the members of the higher and purer understanding of God and his will and power to keep safe, and to save, men from the will of destruction. But such doctrines can be listened to, and received, with all due awe and reverence, and can be received in many things as taught by the old standard; but the immortal race must locate and define the divine spiritual doctrines in a different way from that in which they are taught and believed in by the world. So, then, the doctrines of the prevailing custom of godliness are not contemned nor condemned by the holy doctrines; because each statement, interpretation, word, and formality can be placed in its proper place by the wise and just.

If an associate of the immortal race who is of the world becomes honestly and truly devoted to any one of the holy seed, there shall be no objection to their mingling materially and sociably; for it may be the means of many non-elects becoming elects, by seeing the realities there are in living in harmony with the commandments and teachings of the perfect doctrines. Having in mind and heart a continual thought of life and death, and the suffrages and happiness of man, it gives the complete whole of purity and power to wisdom and understanding, to describe and mark plainly and simply the perils and suffrages which lie under and over the human understanding of the great powers and irresistible forces which are now in the world to lead and compel men to seek the pure life of God, which is now at hand and nigh unto every man's heart and understanding.

Remember and consider that all of you are not prepared to do the same kind of work, nor to pursue the same course; to start at the same time, nor to go in the same direction, even if many of you are to meet at the same Beloved City. The heart of each one is inspired according to his formation and ability, as to the choice of vocation, time, and course to pursue, and what he shall gain if he should start. How can one start unless he has a material guide, and how can there be a material guide unless he is sent, being chosen by, and according to, the glory of almighty power?

"Can a good tree bring forth corrupt fruit, or can a corrupt tree bring forth good fruit? Nay; for by their fruits ye shall know them." You have hereby found and received a material guide, an everlasting friend, an instructor of the true knowledge of God. And this instructor is guided wholly by the seven spirits of almighty power, which are the seven prime doctrinal elements of eternal life, and the gaining of the immortal soul, which purity, laws, and doctrines man transgressed, thereby causing his fall. And you are told by the material guide, the free instructor, that the seven spirits are ruling by the words spoken by the material guide.

Then the material is not the real, but the unseen, which is the seven self-acting mediums of life, which carry man irresistibly on from the mortal life to death, and from death to the resurrection of immortality, the admittance into life eternal. This issue of divine truth outlines the way, marks the journey, declares the conditions, and shows the perils there are from life to death, and from death to the resurrection of the dead, the inheritance of life eternal in the material body. This does not make the material body eternal, but it makes the unseen powers that rule the quickened flesh eternal and pure in all their works, aims, and motives.

I now place by language the seven doctrines of the human soul in every avenue and main street of human thought and intelligence; make the understanding of man consistent with that of divine righteousness; cut inroads into all the desolate countries and vast wildernesses, and make frequent visits into all the secret chambers of sin and iniquity, so that every part of the world that is purged and fully cleansed will rest upon its original and fundamental basis of purity and power in humanity.

This will undoubtedly produce the required necessities, form, and fashion, and reduce to a system, and conform to holy customs of the world, so that spirituality will have a lasting conductor to convey the true wisdom and understanding to the remotest parts of the human world, not allowing the rational mind to rise above nor to go beyond the limits of material things, simply because the spiritual, influential power fills all space of materialism ; for one without the other is not in God, nor is it a complete whole.

The term "psychology," as the title was chosen of God and instilled into the writer to serve technically, means to contain by nature and spirit the entirety of the perfect doctrines of the human soul, which takes in everything that concerns man's eternal salvation spiritually and physically. The seven divisions that constitute the complete whole of "psychology" are the unseen power of Almighty God conferred upon man to use as implements of war to fray out of man the pernicious horns of the uncivilized world, and give in return the horn of the full and perfect salvation. The seven immortal doctrines of "psychology" are the seven divine spirits, the producers of the perfect salvation within the soul of man.

When the revelation of this age is received by men, — I care not who they are, nor what color or talent they have bestowed upon them, — the seven doctrinal spirits begin their involuntary work within the mind and nature, and fathom the inmost thoughts, aims, and intentions, and create understanding as to what is required of men in order that they may begin anew, in life, to lay a new foundation to build upon. When this is done, the seven doctrines give instructions ordinately, day by day, in everything you say, act, do, or perform while about your daily task, and also in all things along the general walks of life.

In the meantime, they do not compel a person to make changes in his mode of living, morally, until he is thoroughly convinced that the natural ways, desires, and aims are injurious to the new life; and also show the injuries, and make plain the successes, there are in turning from the old mode of living.

The fundamental basis while in pursuit of immortality, the beginning of the new life, is the holy exegesis, which interprets day by day the true meaning of Bible language and its many doctrines, which were prepared to suit the different creeds, talents, and vocations of life. The spirit of exegesis will bring to mind, heart, and understanding the proper Scriptures to suit every man's condition, according to the holy purposes of God; which is the agreement between the old and new life pertaining to godliness. The spirit of exegesis is the expositor of all the Scriptures of the apostolic Bible, just as is needed to harmonize with each person's condition and talent. The spirit of exegesis is the great ministering power of pure reasoning, which God sends into the heart of every one who purely and sincerely connects himself with the new life, and is guided by the material guide according to his own desire; and this power of reasoning causes man to think rightly and purely upon the works and acts of God in all things, and keep all other created beings and things on a lower plane than the natural man does. This doctrinal spirit prevents man from exalting himself and other human beings, substances, and creatures above the Almighty God; it causes all things to arise and move upward and downward upon the platform where it was made to exist.

Revelation of the future life is the second ministering spirit with which man is blessed, to teach him all the hidden realities of the new world, and life both old and new; so that his future happiness, and his existence after he is dead to the world, will not be a mystery, as it was to him before he entered into the new life. The doctrinal spirit that expounds the revelation of the future life makes known every hidden secret of sin and purity, also ; uncovers and makes known every privilege that man shall enjoy ; and shows the fulness of human power by the agency of almighty power when man inherits the pure life of Christ, which was promised and given to the just before man's creation. This doctrinal spirit brings man right into the presence of the Supreme, Intelligent Being, where he can be seen as he is, and as he was while performing all of his past work, which was in demonstration of his infinite power. This shows that all these many things God performed and wrought were to create and establish all things needed for man's perfect salvation at the end of the world, which is the end of sin in humanity.

Resurrection of the dead is the third doctrinal spirit, that passes through the bowels of the other doctrines, agrees with every doctrine taught by them, and raises from the dead both good and evil tendencies to make a way for the judgments to be pronounced upon the just and the unjust, so that each kind may be fully rewarded according to their works in humanity. This doctrinal spirit makes known all hidden secrets pertaining to the general resurrection throughout the human world, so that no mystery can conceal itself from this all-searching doctrine. This doctrine stands independently in its world ; and in the meantime flows through the other doctrines, discovers every hidden secret, and causes them to manifest themselves in some way, so that the light of truth, the spirit of burning, and the reflecting word shall throw light upon uncleanness, and consume and make miserable every mite of sin that conceals itself in men's motives and desires, so that unity may exist between motives, aims, and desires in every walk of life.

Salvation of the wicked is the fourth doctrinal spirit, that strives in mental conversation, intelligently and reasonably, to convince the wicked desires and intentions that the things which they are striving blindly to achieve and enjoy are perishable, and cannot find a resting-place anywhere within the limits of the body of death. This doctrine has a continual afflux and reflux from one part of the body to the other, expounding and explaining the real truth to those dispositions which are lying sluggishly around, and wandering vaguely from place to place, unwilling to take part in the fight against sin, nor willing to say a word against the tyranny of sin, nor to take part in the fight against the right. This doctrine convinces the idle neutrals of the happiness and privileges which they shall enjoy if they will turn, heart and soul, and unite with the true doctrines in war against the custom and style of sin, and put down the bondage of sin, which keeps one part of the mind divided against the other. This doctrine stands upon its own base, in its own world, and does an evangelical work throughout the entire world in everything pertaining to spiritual and physical things.

Annihilation of death and hell is the fifth doctrinal spirit, that flows continually through the system of the other doctrines, and destroys all dispositions, aims, and desires that have abandoned all divine and moral laws and doctrines. This doctrine is the utter destruction of the desperate tendencies and desires which cannot, under any circumstances, turn from sin and crime and unite with the just and live for the true life. This doctrine is working with all might and main, from time to time, in every part of the spirit and nature, to slay by vengeance the unrepentant rebels who preside over the mental pit and create all mental disorders and false reasonings which make a person feel, see, and receive the most absurd fallacies, and which cause them to reject and treat with contempt the purest and most rational truth.

Extermination of morality is the sixth doctrinal spirit, that conveys from one part of the world to another those sluggish dispositions that are disinclined to strive to promote the interest of the holy life. This ministering power removes from the mind those mutilated and dead bodies, ruins of cities, animals, and all other creatures that manifest themselves in men's terrible inhuman principles, motives, and desires. This doctrine flows continually through all the other doctrines, clears up all rubbish, and sweeps away all uncleanness and ruins left by the strange acts of the other doctrines, so that the body will not have to continue in dead, loathsome, and mutilated thoughts. This doctrine leaves the mind free from obnoxious odors and trains of thought which issue from rejected and condemned principles. This doctrine prepares the way for the clean and sweet fragrance of transhumanity, which can only exist where purity and sincerity reign ; and if anything aside from this should by chance steal into the soul, transhumanity fades away like a rose during a warm day, when plucked from its bower.

Transhumanity is the seventh doctrinal division, a serenely ministering spirit, which is free from all wrath, roughness, or anything that burdens or tends to unhappiness. It rules and exists in the land of rest only, which is prepared for the people who have overcome all trials and temptations of that wicked one who arises while passing from life to death (which is the world), and from death to the resurrection of the dead, the inheritance of transhumanity in the material body. This all-seeing doctrine raises the whole being above everything that tends to hatred, deception, injury, or any small or great tendencies in man that oppose the welfare of others in any way. This doctrine, when fully established in the heart of man, will surely and undoubtedly keep out every evil thought, desire, aim, and motive, so that nothing but pure civilization and purity can reign in the land of transhumanity, which is the end of the terrible judgments and the wrath of God against the sinful spirit and nature, and, at last, the end of the world in man, who was very envious against Almighty God while performing his strange work for the redemption of his elect.

As it is by the fulness of the pure word of God that Christ is to make his appearance to the world, and cause his life to be received, honored, and adored above all other things, it is the abundance of word that shall bring about and make manifest the real life of Christ. And where the abundance of word prevails, there will the truth also reign ; and the Holy Spirit will move over the surface of word and truth to give vent to wisdom and understanding, by which the immortal soul is to gain access into the perfect rest, which is the domain which the human soul has long labored and struggled, in faith, to achieve.

The human soul is laboring, from time to time, to reach entity, — a sure and unchangeable habitation, — as surely as men seek to obtain their own property in the temporal world. As long as the human soul dwells within the limits of the body of death, there can be no staid joy, peace, and contentment, because it is a wayfarer and a sojourner in some unknown world where the struggle for liberty shall cease.

Well, how is this journey made, and by what source of power is man to be carried to reach his long-sought-for home? Man is to sail upon the great waters of divine word, spirit, and truth.

The Word is the great waters, the Truth is the ship, and the Holy Spirit is the propelling power that produces speed and irresistible motion ; and by receiving the word, spirit, and truth in the entirety, just as revealed from heaven, you are thereby permitted to enter upon the great waters and begin the journey without knowing or seeking to know what time you are to land, or what storm shall come against you while making the journey.

There is no danger of being lost nor of running into perils that you cannot conquer while you remain upon the immense waters, for the pilot knows all the perilous places and obstructions along the way, and he knows the time and seasons when storms are most numerous and violent ; for many a time has he piloted the ship into the harbor on the other side of this world.

Remember that you are natural-born slaves to the commandments of your own sinful nature, the leading customs and styles of this world, as much as a child is supposed to be subject to the teachings of its parents, whether good or evil teachings. And you can no more be the sons of God in reality, while you live to the glory and honor of your own nature, which is the sinful world, than you can take ore and make an axe or a shovel without carrying the substance that produces iron through the proper process.

You are enslaved to the sins of this world, and you are also the slaves of righteousness in the world, if you are connected with any faith in the name of godliness. And your faith and works in the world in the name of godliness will profit you no more than the sinners' who have never entered the faith, if you fail to partake of the doctrines of the second coming of Christ. Then there is no more reward to be given to the so-called righteous than to the so-called unrighteous in the world, unless the so-called Christians receive the perfect words of God. And if those who have lived unrighteously in the sight of men should partake of the perfect doctrines, they would be receiving the righteousness of the first and second coming of Christ combined, and God would confer upon them the perfection and the understanding of both ages, while they would not be slaves to sin nor righteousness, but would be the chosen seed of God, according to the glory and honor of righteousness ; which seed shall live above the cursed law, having the Cross of Christ for their foundation, which cannot be removed, and having, also, the duties and curses which were under the law for their ramparts and door of admittance into eternal rest, peace, and pleasure.

The heirs of the perfect age shall not look vainly and unreasonably to the righteousness and recompense which were promised to those who have labored in vain, according to their own desires and understanding, to enter into eternal happiness by living subject to the laws and doctrines of the Cross ; for the many things which were hitherto written were the many inroads paved out in the sinful world to lead men on to the perfect world, that they may reach the plains of felicity, a land where darkness and perils have no place.

The question has often been asked, and it has been duly considered by many who have heard of their claim ; but it has never been answered satisfactorily in words nor thoughts, because God saw fit heretofore to keep it concealed from the untaught world, just as he has kept many things that were not best to divulge until the fulness of the times when everything that is hidden shall be revealed, and that which is covered shall be uncovered.

Whether things are concealed or known, all things belonging to the glorification of God and the salvation of men have worked and performed all things just proper for God's determination, now and henceforth. Not one jot of his workings has been in vain, neither is one tendon of the mortal and immortal soul out of its proper place. Just as everything now is, so was it created to be, and so will it carry out its work as it was created and commissioned to do without very much struggle.

I must name the complete whole of these truths, revelations, and doctrines, so that its name be known far and near ; and this will cause the wonder to cease among those who have sought to know the full meaning of all of these things. These truths, revelations, and doctrines, whose author and members are living under and guided by them, do not come under the name of any particular creed, faith, opinion, nor religion; but they are, namely, the chosen seed of the living God, the heirs of the highest salvation according to God's glory and honor in all things, that they may bring others to the same state.

The author and members of these doctrines are not antagonistic against any creed or faith that is tending to godliness, or that would like to. They are only antagonistic against those things that produce and maintain sin. And everything that promotes the true comfort for all men is revealed and supported to reach the people aright.

The evil craves and desires of sin, which is man's worst enemy, are seated in humanity, and prevail in the spirit of man; and these must be cast out and consumed by being renounced upon oath, in order that man may gain what he lost. The question is, What is it that man lost, and what is there for him to gain? Man lost the power which he had over sin and uncleanness; and now he must regain dominion, by the supreme power of truth and understanding, over every sinful crave and desire, and all such things must be exiled from nature and spirit.

This will make man think, act, judge, and desire differently in all things. When this is done, man will cease from being angry with and envious against his fellow man, and will cease from striving falsely and maliciously against one another for competition and excellency. But as long as the prince of this world makes laws, conceives doctrines, invents patents and styles, according to his glory, for man to strive to obtain, so long will sin reign over the true life, wisdom, and the Gospel of God. The true Gospel must make its own laws, and declare its own doctrines, and stick to its own principles, and invent its own customs and styles, and rule in everything.

The next thing is to tell where man shall receive the full blessings and privileges which are promised to the heirs of the perfect salvation. Man lost the power of pure righteousness which God gave him over sin and unclean things ; and he must be enjoying a material and spiritual existence in the temporal world in order to be restored to perfect holiness and happiness, as he was when created. Then man's reward and perfect salvation are to take place in the temporal world materially and spiritually ; and without this privilege and blessing the final redemption and recompense of man are not finished. For if man is utterly deprived of earthly necessities such as are needed to make life materially happy, he is not fully restored to perfection ; for the material and spiritual prosperity must work together in order to realize happiness.

Man has already, and can leave behind him, the real necessities of life, in order to please God and to fulfil his determinations, and to reach that degree of power where he could give up the world for the true life to come into him and rule over the world. But such is not yet the perfection and fulness of salvation, nor can it ever be until man is blessed with both the temporal and the spiritual necessities of life, and in the meantime causes the spiritual to rule over the temporal, and uses it as not abusing it in every sense of justice and purity. The world must first be shut out, and purged by the true laws and Gospel of God ; which will cause the resurrection of saints and sinners, to bring them to justice and judgment in answer to the deeds done in the bodies of men.

After all this has taken place, you are then justified and sustained in looking for a new heaven and a new earth wherein dwelleth pure righteousness. But before this comes to pass, you see, behold, and realize the world within, which was your first heaven, on fire, and realize that the works therein are being destroyed by fire. This is the place where the soul loses all hope of entering the rest which remains for the people of God.

After the works and sins of the world are renounced and consumed, the revealing unto you of a new life, doctrines, and privileges is the time when hope revives, which causes the soul to look diligently for a new heaven (which is a new life and trust) and a new earth (which is a cleansed body), where the true righteousness of God will dwell forever; where the glory of the earthly will be equally as great, in comparison, as that of the heavenly. For then everything will be in God's image and likeness; and God will be in all things, above all things, under all things, and will rule over all things according to his glory and honor, and men's peace, pleasure, and happiness.

In speaking or writing of the spiritual world and body, God used the same language and terms to describe its many wonders as it took to describe the great wonders of the temporal world. The soul is a spiritual body, and its substance and building are composed of pure and plain language; and the world in which the soul lives and reigns is the same.

In order to describe the reign of the soul, and the infinitive existence of the world in which the immortal soul lives and reigns, God saw fit to use the same language and terms of description and limitation as he did to describe and limit the happiness and privileges there are in the temporal world, where godly power and purity once reigned.

Having seen that all of these many things that have long been taught, spoken of, and thought upon are unseen, and never can be seen as men look and hope for it to be accomplished, there has come a time when they shall know the truth of the whole matter as pertaining to life and death, peace, joy, and happiness, the resurrection of the life of God, and the final coming of Christ to reign over all sin and uncleanness in the human soul and body.

This brings about the whole change concerning the abolishment of death and the establishment of life immortal, the resurrection and the life of the saints who live and are dead within the beings and nature of men who are now in existence materially on earth. And none of the saints who have passed out of their fleshly habitations during the past ages of the world have yet entered the perfect rest; neither have they entered into the perfect heaven, where God lives and reigns most gloriously and immortally. They have not reached a world and life happier and purer than this present world and its members of integrity. They are dead, living, and sleeping; but they are not one whit better situated than the so-called Christians of this present world; and they will not enter into the perfect heaven and rest until the general resurrection, which must work secretly in every material saint, which will undoubtedly bring the once material but now spiritual saints into the general judgments. Then they will progress up from the sins and crimes of the finite kingdoms, just as the material bodies progress in thought, knowledge, and deeds with which they live and reign. There are some who are higher than others, because of their faith and works in the sinful kingdoms; and there are some who will progress much faster than others, because their faith, works, and tendencies differ in quality and value, which makes the difference in progress.

The second coming of Christ means the second coming of the supreme divine laws and doctrines to reign eternally over sin, death, and hell in every one who receives Christ as he is. The resurrection of the dead and the general judgments against the wicked mean to raise from the dead the truths, laws, doctrines, and true principles which have fallen asleep in humanity, and which are the saints coming into judgment to receive their recompense, so as to enter into the perfect rest, which is their eternal home.

With all my might and main, I have used the best and purest words of God to show and prove to the world two great questions, which are life and death, and to show how death and life must come to all. But I fear that the habitual understanding of these things, and the inherited superstition of life and death will be too strong for some to understand the true way and enter into life. For this reason I am compelled to dwell upon the most important question, so as to remove the greatest obstruction, the concealed stumbling-stone.

By the Cross, all the so-called Christians have been crucified and deprived of the real life and knowledge of God, even as the material Cross slew the figurative Jesus Christ, and deprived him of a material entity. Why? Because the material enemies who invented the material Cross were too strong for him in that day, and were desperately opposed to a life so pure as his ; and for this reason they had power to slay him, that his life should not reign over them to change their sinful laws and customs, which were deeply rooted in their nature, and occupied all space in spirit.

By the spiritual cross and enemies the heirs of Christ are overpowered and killed all the day long. And the same sinful powers that fought against the figurative Jesus Christ in days of old are embodied to-day in material bodies, in rejecting and unbelieving tendencies ; and these are crucifying Christ by rejecting his word, truth, and spirit, which is now his real being. Why is this evil allowed to prevail? Because this is the method to try the good, and destroy the evil love, honor, and affections which men have for the natural world and its belongings.

After man is dead from the sting of the Cross, its continual presence cannot bring misery and woe, as it did when man was alive to the dread of the Cross. You see, and understand, that the Cross is the annihilator of the mortal man, whose pleasure and hope are centered in the world, so that he cannot do the things he would if he could break the sweet influence of the world. Therefore the Cross must continue until every tender tie is destroyed, and all feelings of hope and trust in this world are passed away.

When you reach this degree of power, which seems to be altogether weakness, you are then empowered and supplied with the spirit of confidence in God's word to hope beyond the natural world, using the continual presence of the Cross for your sure trust, foundation, and rock of defence, whereby you have the assurance of that everlasting hope of eternal life and perfect dominion over the enemies of this world who bring the Cross upon you, while the powers that are evil and working with you are reared up and slain. The things within you that are evil, when they are slain, leaving you with a broken and hopeless spirit, are not to your hurt, but to your final triumph over the brutal powers that bring the Cross.

When all powers that are subject to the penalties of the Cross are slain, the Cross is no more a cross, nor a place of offence, but your glory, praise, rest, peace, comfort, and reconciliation with God, who redeemed you to himself, a praise and endless glory. Then without the Cross there could be no death nor life after death; for you are told that death must come by the Cross, and life by death; and the works of the perfect salvation issue from life, which comes after death. Well, then, shall they seek the Cross, or make one for themselves and fellow creatures, that death may come speedily? Oh no; for God never ordained that this should be.

The Cross, in many instances, comes through those whom you trust as friends; and again, from those looked upon as enemies ; and again, you make your own cross, sometimes wilfully ; and again, it is brought about by the voluntary powers, the demands of your own selfish desires and imaginations, which creep secretly into your mind and create things that have no weight nor foundation ; which will bear rule over true reasoning and common sense as long as the false is received and the true understanding is contemned.

Again, the Cross comes to you from things and from a source with which you never expected to be crossed, and from things that are entirely unreasonable, and from things that you were naturally disinclined to do ; and such things you are liable to be accused of doing, which is fully strong enough to destroy your will, way, and desires, until you are dead universally.

When I say universally, it applies to your selfish love, hope, and desires, which must be dead from everything and every person on earth ; and you then have no hope but life eternal, and that is void until God confers upon you his spirit of hope, and then it is not you that hope, love, and desire, but the hope of God manifested in you. Then God will walk in you, teach in you, talk in you, love in you, desire in you, and take pleasure in you to do his will ; while you cannot possibly have a desire nor anything pertaining to it of yourself.

God's Spirit will lead his temple in all things to do his perfect will in all ways of peace, safety, prosperity, and happiness, where no evil can befall you in anything that you shall see fit to go into, or to assign your heart and hands to do. For the wicked are dead, and are as the dust under your feet, which you tread down thoughtlessly, and are powerless over you. Here you have entered into an endless day, an unchangeable peace, and an untarnishable purity, where the river of the water of life ebbs continually to keep pure and alive the tree of life, that it may yield its life-giving fruits to give life to those who are dead to life, having no part in life eternal further than mercy seeth fit to measure and bestow upon them according to their sincerity, pleasure, and devotion to the perfect truths.

If there should be any who are unable to partake of life as freely as they would, because of the powerful opponents of nature, and cannot possibly advance in the growth of power and wisdom as fast as others, it is unwise to reproach them, or to bring a railing accusation against them ; for it is wiser and purer to bear with them — peradventure they might be made able to withstand the evil powers, and unite with their advanced fellow creatures.

There are others who may have started the journey from the natural life to death, to enter into life eternal, and after beginning the journey find themselves unprepared, and are unable to stem the powers of their natural creation and condition ; and in the meantime they find it best and wisest to revolt from living to the glory and honor of life immortal, and live within the bounds of their formation and construction, bordering on the laws and doctrines of morality as near as their tendencies will allow and grant life and prosperity.

I write these words and leave them as a sign for neutrals to judge and decide upon which life is best and most prosperously suited for them to live, wherefrom they can obtain the most peace and satisfaction.

All things pertaining to the natural world and the resurrection of life immortal should be performed rationally in all things, — by doing those things that are most expedient for peace with men and reconciliation with God ; by placing yourself in that position where both God and man will be best pleased with your talent and works. It is not always wise and just to do or assert things which you know will create strife or enemies, even though your motives are solely to do good, since there are many ways to avoid such, by waiting and enduring until your opponent is taken out of the way. In other cases, it is wise to urge a matter, even though strife should follow, where the welfare of some special good is to be sacrificed by waiting.

To make the matter short, I would add : in all things, work to support and preserve the right, I care not whether it brings strife, death, peace, or division. When you stand for the right, stand wholly so, for there is always victory and safety where the right prevails. Here is the evil, and here is the right ; well, the right is wholly right, and the wrong is wholly wrong. This is very true, but in many cases the right can step across the bounds of right and enter upon the premises of wrong, thus making a breach of trespass.

The right has crossed the boundary of extremity in opposition of the wrong ; and, right here, right and justice stand in defence of the wrong, and mingle with the wrong to deal with equity. That which is purely right must follow up the principles and perfection of right, if it crosses over and stands in defence of the basest sin and crime, where justice and discretion have not been done.

There are many things you can do that would be strictly moral to the worldly man, but would be defiant to the true teachings of godliness. What would be defiant to one godly person's progress might not be defiant to another, because what would retard the spiritual progress of one person would not affect another in the least ; and what would be obnoxious to a person at one time would be productive of life at another, after he has passed through the scourge and is permitted to take in the comforts of life universally.

There is no sin nor uncleanness in anything that God created for the good of man, except at certain times, when he is told to deny them for a purer and more lasting good. Then if man should obey willingly, in doing the things which God will have him to do at the proper time, there is no such thing as God's withholding any good from him when he seeth that he is worthy of it, and stands in need of it, and that the return of these things to man will be for his betterment according to God's glory. When you endure trials willingly, your reward comes speedily ; but if you oppose the will wilfully, with murmuring and strife, you turn away and reject your own reward, and shut the door of mercy and victory against you.

The most striking and essential interest of man is rational godliness, leaving out all superstition of future punishment and happiness ; because it is universally known that the prevailing ideas, opinions, and fearful superstitions concerning future punishment and happiness are preposterous in every degree of common sense. And even if such things could ever be as they are hideously described by false teachers and preachers, is it possible for the fearful superstition to exempt men from wrath and punishment, and assure them safety or grant them the privilege of entering into life eternal without having any knowledge of it, nor of how it is to come ?

All the many things which men proclaim, bearing on future punishment and happiness, are to be fulfilled in many, but not as men conceive it as a rule ; for they will never see as they look, nor as they expect, nor as they hear, neither will these things take place as they have defined them. Still, they will come to pass to make man just what he should be in honor of the perfect life.

The whole change of man, entering into the perfect life, and being doomed into misery and woe, is to take place within the soul and material body while the body exists upon the earth. The change, which is death, — to leave the world, to enter into life eternal, and yet to exist in the world materially,— is to take place within the soul.

Leaving the world behind, as a sacrifice, is sure death to the mortal being, whose hope, trust, and pleasure are grafted in the sinful world; and death is the only power to force the mortal to desert the world, which it has loved and adored since mankind began to multiply the improvements upon the earth. It places the immortal soul in a world of irresistible power, where the mortal soul must break its mighty hold from the world, and be cast down to darkness and death, to be consumed by suffering under the just laws and doctrines of the immortal soul, which has struggled so long to obtain the ever-ruling sceptre, to keep away from the tree of life, and to slay the fatness and ravin of sin. Well, could the mortal being have done differently to shun the punishment now due to him as a just recompense?

I shall not enter into suppositions; I shall dwell upon the things that have been, those which now are, and those which shall be hereafter. If things had been different from what they are to-day, I would have dwelt upon the main situation, even as I am now dwelling upon the present conditions of things. The world has a breach which is incurable by the members of the world; and for this reason I must devote my time and understanding to the condition of things which are thickly covered and well hidden from the view of men. If a man has committed a terrible crime, it is folly to argue upon what would be the outcome had it not taken place : the case is to try him for crime, and punish him for crime.

The world, which is the people at large as they exist, has a rupture which the people cannot bind up nor heal; because the corruption that exists in the world has come to the fulness, so that peace can no longer be preserved until there is a scourge, and each person has his just due, whether it is success or failure.

The wrongs enacted against the rights of the just in the world have become so very obnoxious that the right shall no longer defend nor sympathize with wrong-doers, who have caused all the ruptures in the world. There can be no binding up of the breach, for the world must see what the world contains, so that the right will stand only for the right, and overthrow the tyranny of sin. Sin has reigned throughout all ages of the world, and the time and season have come for the right to reign over wrong-doers and bring them to judgment and justice ; therefore, sin is wrathful, and it is being dethroned, and cast down to humility, misery, and death, to suffer for its detestable works against the right.

The world has reached that platform where natural brotherhood can no longer combine successfully, nor can love have a resting-place in each other's breast ; because the days of natural brotherhood are far spent, and the immortal brotherhood must come in and put an end to the false. This puts a higher duty and responsibility upon every man to accept another thought of life which is higher and deeper than the present ruling thoughts, which only irritate and throw the world into a worse chaos and the turmoiling of nations.

How is man to break away and free himself from the rupture of the world, and enter into the world of new thoughts and genius, since all men are associated with the world to some extent, and one man's failure affects another, and they are all linked in talent, trade, and profession, that one may rightly support the other, and save each man his fellow creature ?

The physical world and its laws and doctrines are the temple for the spiritual to dwell in, in peace and safety. The true spiritual shall rule over the temporal, in order to dwell in the temporal as happily as it is enjoying freedom in the spiritual ; while the true spiritual and temporal shall undoubtedly overpower the falsities which are desperately opposing the spiritual and physical laws and doctrines, and bring the true spiritual and temporal together, so that one will rightly support the other, and keep out the stringent and unjust laws and doctrines. In order to bring this about, there is no way to avoid a terrible breach, which, after a long struggle, is compelled to bring in everlasting peace, justice, and happiness. Then sufferings and a mighty rupture are the only alternatives through which true brotherly love and unceasing unity are to come, so that the false and the pure no longer mingle.

I now state, in answer to the question concerning how man is to free himself from the disrupture of the sinful world, and from being subject to the turmoiling of nations, that if peace, justice, discretion, and conscientiousness are hovering about your breast, and your essential aims and desires are to make peace and give each man his due, and yet, in spite of all this, you find that your works are contemned and utterly rejected by the corrupt members of the world ; if you have done all that can be done, and made all attempts to bring the members of the world under the government of peace and justice, yet find your works of no avail, you are justified, qualified, and blessed forever in deserting them entirely, and living the life which you know to be just, not allowing yourself to mingle with their modes of living and teaching any further than it agrees with your knowledge of right.

You can live in peace, materially, right among those who are false swearers, contentious, and subject to lying, tattling, and disputing, and yet take no part in their corruption. This is done that the power of the Almighty may speedily bring them to justice and repentance, to suffer for the pleasure which they have taken against the righteousness of God.

You are a material being, and you live in a material world,

and the material necessities of life to sustain your body materially must come from the world, through the members of the world, whether they are supporters of the right or creators of evil. You are not supposed, nor are you required, to live a hermit's life materially, by living in utter seclusion from the world; but you can seclude yourself from those wrongs and injustices practised by the members who are grafted in the world and have no other thoughts, aims, nor desires, working within the range of common sense, to rise above the characteristics and the understanding of the world.

Though you can move, perform, work, and deal with and among the members of the world, still there are a few things which you and they cannot have brotherly mutuality in; and you who are of the righteousness and wisdom of the eternal world have a perfect right to stand steadfast in your profession, as boldly as does the world in its trust and profession. They trust, hope, and enjoy the life of the world, and they are not ashamed to proclaim it, and to disregard and contemn the righteousness of God as he has made it manifest in the chosen seed, according to his glory. So you who are of the household of the royal family of Christ, in honor of his first and second coming to reign over and destroy the works of sin in all who receive him, have as much boldness and authority, mingled with independence, to stand firm in your trust, hope, and life in the same — as much as the members of the world are commissioned by sin to stand dexterously in support of their faith.

If the righteousness of God, which is life eternal and dominion over all wrongs, is the seat of your life, the immovable foundation upon which you stand, the antagonism of the world is mere trash to you. But if you stand in awe of the members of the world simply because you fear their power, which you feel above you, take this as a sure sign that you are one of the subjects of the world, and are opposing, deceitfully, your own life; and know that the very same works and principles of the world are slumbering within you, awaiting an opportunity to mingle with their kind, where they can enjoy the realities of life. Wrath and curses, disappointment of aims and desires, will dwell with that person if he is mingling with the just, until he is allowed the privilege of mingling with his kind.

If a person is pursuing a course in opposition to his controlling pleasure, understanding, and desire, he may abide for years under the shadow of the perfect truths, but the time will come when he will be compelled to succumb to the life which he is best suited to live; or he will make it known in some way that he is not striving to obtain the things which he desires most of all. Above all things, in this thought, seek and strive to obtain those things in which you take most pleasure, and to which you can give your time and talent, to serve easily, faithfully, and pleasurably, as long as they are things in the moral world. If you desire and can take pleasure in wealth, seek it earnestly; if an husband or wife, seek such earnestly; if an education, fame, pleasure, or splendor, seek it earnestly; and if your desire, taste, and pleasure are centered in pure godliness, as pure as that of which I write, seek it earnestly, and do not allow anything else to take first rank in your heart. Choose those good things, or those tending to good, that you know are first in your thoughts and pleasure, when it dwells within the sphere of civilization; for this is the thing that God prefers you to do; and you will prosper at it if you are loyal to all the true principles that support it and make it a talent, trade, or pleasure.

The time has arrived to brood over the laws of true reasoning, to show the origin of false reasoning, to dwell upon the principal resources of perfect and unceasing success, which must pass through the loins of true thinking powers to obtain

48

the true wisdom, and to depart from all baneful evils which come
through the bowels of false reasoning,— the decision given upon
matters of a hurtful nature.

If a thing is of a pernicious character, and cannot be other-
wise, it is the power of true reasoning — which must produce
truth, and which is understanding — to depart from it. If a
person or thing is pure and true in the acclamation of its
authenticity, it is the power of false reasoning that changes or
establishes the opinion of a person to reject and turn from it. It
is the mere words of true reasoning that bring the spirit and its
joyful truths to the soul of the man who believes in every true
way and principle of life. And it is the absurdity of false reasoning that brings the spirit of grief, heaviness, and, lastly, firm
unbelief to the soul, which appears in the form of the true
words of God, and which issues from the bottomless pit, the
prince of revenge and desperation.

In order to deceive you, the wise and lettered prince of sin
uses the most practical schemes to get into false reasoning, by
bringing to your minds the words of God. After you have
received the words and trusted in such as proceeding from the
true source, you are offered the false, which you are liable to
receive without carefully examining it ; and in a short time you
could not receive nor believe the truth if you desired to. The
living and rational words of God, in their tenor of wisdom and
understanding, are given as the only way in which Christ is to
be received into the soul ; and if the words of truth are rejected,
it is because the words of sin are believed and received into the
heart according to your own inferior understanding of right and
wrong. When you receive the false words, you receive false
reasoning ; and when you receive false reasoning, you receive
the Devil's spirit ; and when you reject the true for the false,
you cannot of yourself cast it out and receive the true spirit at

your own wishes. Then you must wait for the return of the Holy Spirit to cast out your enemy, who is too strong for you; and then you may suffer, while waiting, more than you ever expected, after contemning the true word and spirit wilfully.

If all that promotes happiness and prosperity must come through true reasoning, hearing, understanding, and receiving the words of truth, then the words of truth are of more value than they have ever been prized in the mind, and they should be looked at, and esteemed in the heart as highly as they are worthy and important; because the pure word of God is the only source of power prepared to make man immortal in thought and principle, is the mediator between God and man, and, lastly, is God himself, who dwells in different forms, and has many divisions flowing from his Omnipresent Being.

All crime and uncleanness, which dug the burning metal pit, the terrible disorders of the mind, proceeded from the false word in the likeness of true reasoning and understanding of things,— the judging of right and wrong. The false words that bring mighty false reasoning should be more desperately and powerfully opposed when they begin their spurious work in the soul.

How do the false and the true reasoning begin their work in the mind? There was a time when you knew nothing of these truths and claims, while you had no thought whatever concerning them. Until you heard, you could think nothing; and when you heard, the sound came to you in the form of words.

What set you to thinking after this had taken place? You heard something that you did not understand, and this produced a wonderment in your mind, because you never heard of anything like it before.

"The idea of a man claiming to do the work that you claim can be done is preposterous," you say. You may say, then, that you don't believe it. He who allows himself to go so far as to say even so much as I have stated above has accepted a regiment of false reasoners,— the council of the Devil's kingdoms,— which bring to pass the words of the Lord, saying: "But these, as natural brute beasts, made to be taken and destroyed, speak evil of the things that they understand not; and shall utterly perish in their own corruption."

Suppose you had said, when you entered into a wonderment after hearing the strange report: "I am a believer in the works of God in whatever form he may appear; and, knowing not in what way he shall appear to reveal and give himself to mankind in the perfect degree of his life, I shall not condemn nor receive until I appeal to God for understanding of this strange report."

After you have received instruction that it proceeds from God for the welfare of mankind when the world reaches that plain of purity where it can receive the true doctrine, love it, adore and enjoy it above all things, you next find out, surely, whether or not it is what you need; and if you have no further knowledge in honor of it imparted to you, to lead you nearer to receive it, do not partake of it of yourself; for you are to continue as you were before hearing of it, and to wait your chance a future day, that you may be made ready to partake of its truths.

If you never have a controlling desire leading you to take hold of its truths and manner of living, change not from what you first sought to know, and were duly informed,— that these writings came from God. And if you are not a believer in the workings of godliness, allow not yourself to discourse upon nor to judge matters of that nature; for it will never bless, help, nor elevate any one to speak evil of the righteousness of God, nor to judge what he does not understand regarding the truth.

When you pursue the true course, which I have briefly outlined in honor of the truth, rest assured that you are in the swiftest current of godly reasoning; and if you pursue any other course to obtain the righteousness of Christ, understand and know that you are in the channel of false reasoning.

If you are not a subject for the service of divine truth, and you can never understand anything concerning its method of work, it will be of no loss to you; for God, through Christ, knew your condition, and saw fit to leave you afar off, and kept the understanding of these things from your reach, which was for your present and future good. If you had taken hold of the divine doctrines, and were unable to stem the trials which would arise above your strength by being subject to its teachings, your condition, because you had taken hold of what you could not receive in full, would be far worse than it would have been had you never undertaken the journey.

When a new good is evil spoken of, it becomes prevalent, because people do not fully understand its motive and purposes, and are not wise enough to pursue an honorable course regarding it; hence they exercise their own opinion, to pacify their own curiosity. Those who are weak in sentiments will gasp and fight desperately in defence of the prevailing opinion, and will not accept any opinion of their own, though, in the outset, they had a good and true opinion of it, until they heard the opinion of some one or more whom they looked upon as being their superiors in judging any matter.

If you are a man or woman, and not legally subject to any one's power and opinion, you are supported and justified, in the sight of Christ, in being your own judge according to Christ's inspiration working within you, which supplies you with the sincere thought as to what manner of words you shall believe, or what manner you shall disbelieve. If there was a perfect established doctrine anywhere on earth, this would not have to be so.

There is none ; and for this reason, you and all others are wait-ing for the coming of the perfect truths, the dawning of the eternal day, to overrule the darkness and inspire your hearts with the perfect knowledge, the understanding of Christ as he lives and reigns with God in the highest heaven — so far above you foolish creatures, who feel yourselves so very important in his sight. So, if you have heard or read of these truths, it will be wise on your part to wait patiently before you receive or reject ; for in the end it will be to your advantage, and also where you are situated now, without hope or desire to believe or understand. You did not create yourself, neither will you change yourself ; but you can be a reasonable thinking man even where you are.

Evil speakers, men who are prejudiced in any respect, false reasoners, and haters of the right shall have their part with those who regard not the truth in any sense, even though they knew that it was the truth. I write not for those who would not accept the right even if they had an opportunity to receive the true doctrines of life ; but in support of those who would, if they knew the true way, and had some one to be true to them in helping them to rise above the unjust, who keep them sub-ject to their wicked devices simply because their natural require-ments of life come through their antagonists. It is so fixed and decreed that the just shall hereafter live in support of the just, irrespective of being dependent on the unjust, that they may not live as they have been allowed to through the past ages of the world. You know very well that if you are subject to your enemies for the sustenances of life, you are compelled to swerve from the right in many cases, in order to have your tem-poral needs supplied ; but if you are independent in every sense, you are all-powerful in the human world, and will prevail in every degree of right.

I have seen and beheld Satan in the finite world in every form, degree, and claim in which men exist in the world — not only in imitation of the so-called realities of truth, righteousness, and justice, but as real as the purity of the world ever was or now is; and I find that the whole machinery is intermingling with sin and vice — the schemes of the Devil — in religion, wisdom, refinement, learning, wealth, love, honor, sacrifices, and everything that pretends to be incorruptible and for the betterment of mankind, that man, by living righteously, may glorify his God, who decreed man's formation and production.

I do not say that many do not strive, in every profession of good existing, to obtain immortality in their works, in honor of the true life; but they have failed to attain that state of purity and power. You are the heirs of immortality by faith in the life of Christ; and you can only be made heirs in reality by receiving the full Gospel of Christ,— not according to your own zeal and knowledge, but according to chances, the blessed invitations which God, through Christ, shall place in your hand and heart. And this chance, when placed within your reach, is not to be used selfishly, but with all self-denying desires and works, looking wholly to the pleasure of Christ, and his knowledge and understanding, and to the interests of your fellow creatures, who are involved in the same blessed calling.

If you live, act, and work to this end of purity, God will, through Christ, raise up friends to care for you; and your needs will be supplied without your taking thought thereof. Where there is so much thought of self, and how self is to be remunerated, there is no good done for your fellow creatures. He who worketh for mere self worketh in vain, unto destruction; and he who worketh for his fellow creatures findeth treasures of reward and never-ceasing friends. Above all things in this degree of knowledge, keep your works and motives out of the baneful current of self, and you will be compelled to prosper.

The very next important discourse, and the termination of this issue of "The Lamb's Book of Life" in support of the manifest power of the holy truths, is to show that the customary learning of men in the world has not yet outwitted the craft of the lawless; which craft did not come to them through the customary system of learning, but by nature's own inventions, through natural science, and through schemes of deviltry. This craft is improving and perfecting its art and wisdom every moment.

My immovable theme is : if the wicked, with their mean and brutal devices, which they keep concealed among their kind, can succeed and prosper for a time, then why can not the unrevealed and unsystematical righteousness of God — which is concealed and working in the chosen seed, and which is given to redeem mankind — be prudent enough in the perfect right to outwit the normally educated of the sinful world, and perform many good things among its kind in secret, and among men of the world, for the final redemption of those who believe in presenting their bodies an eternal and acceptable sacrifice unto God, to use in all things to his rational glory and honor, according to his finished purposes? Thus the final redemption of all mankind who believe firmly in pure righteousness and equity may be realized and enjoyed, instead of being proclaimed falsely, in wisdom of words which come from men of vain conceit, who take pleasure in their own display, in fancy idolatry, that they may obtain the highest praise of men, which confers upon them a rich reward for their faithful efforts.

You who are the chosen seed cannot strive solely for men's admiration and commendation, lest you lose track of the honor and praise of him who inspired you with wisdom and power, to gain to you a glory and praise. Glory and praise are what every

man of right, who is faithful to his calling and true to the principles which erect and uphold the office which he holds, should
have. But in the life and calling of the holy seed, the entire
glory is given to God involuntarily, and he confers the same upon
his faithful children, who seek not their own glory, but the
glory of him who conformed them, by his own creation, to his
honor, that they may reign in his life by his power over the
many wrongs of this world, and rise above those charms which
take hold upon the children of darkness, who are. reserved for
this purpose, — that the workers of good may see and know the
reward of the unjust.

In ages to come the world will pass out of the stages of sin
and crime, and enter into the perfect day, where the perfection
of the right shall keep clean and pure all men whose desires and
aims are to do good and to make others to know every sinew of
sin and every tendon of right. This can only and shall only be
done by each person's keeping the blessed secrets of the perfect
good concealed from the antagonists of the right, and by not
allowing them to pry into his life and mode of living ; this is
the only successful way to life, and no other way will ever reach
the desired end. Hence it is useless to make open declaration
of all of your aims and intentions to the unbelieving world, as
long as your own conscience is free from condemnation, and your
whole being means to live and strive to obtain and perform the
right in all things.

If you should step across the bounds of right, it will not be
you, but the pleasure of God working in your members to use
you an instrument to measure to some wicked one his just due.
Well, then, some wicked one may ask, " Why, if a thing is true and
good, do you keep it concealed from the world ? " The following
standards God has raised up to support you :   " But when thou
doest alms, let not thy left hand know what thy right hand

doest." "Give not that which is holy unto the dogs, neither cast ye your pearls before swine, lest they trample them under their feet, and turn again and rend you. "

Why is it that some people, in order to be redeemed from the pollutions of the world, are required and compelled to make a spiritual and material sacrifice of this world's goods which they claim as their own, while another can retain his belongings and still make a holy sacrifice which would be acceptable to the Divine Spirit ? The man who has to give this world's goods over to utter destruction is compelled to do so because the things of this world are his god, which is idolized in his heart, and his whole being is corrupted thereby. And for this reason, in order to inherit immortality and be redeemed from the terrible venoms of sin, his vain gods that are no gods must be dethroned, and his idols entirely destroyed ; while the man who does not think more highly than he should of this world's goods is not affected very deeply by the pollutions of the world, and in the meantime, his worldly goods are not destroyed, but given over to an increase.

Well, how shall the different characters be distinguished one from another, since both claim to have the same love and taste for the pure life of Christ ? The following standards are revealed to distinguish the false from the true : " I am come a light into the world, that whosoever believeth on me should not abide in darkness." "And if any man hear my words and believe not, I judge him not : for I came not to judge the world, but to save the world." "He that rejecteth me, and receiveth not my words, the words that I have spoken, the same shall judge him in the last day."

Again it is written, to substantiate the eternal truth : " When he is come, he will reprove the world of sin, and of righteousness, and of judgment : of sin, because they believe not on me ;

of righteousness, because I go to my father, and ye see me no more ; of judgment, because the prince of this world is judged."

I have yet many things to say unto you, but ye cannot hear them now. Howbeit, when he, the Spirit of truth, is come, he will guide you into all truth ; for he shall not speak of himself, but whatsoever he shall hear, that shall he speak, and he will show you things to come. He shall glorify me ; for he shall receive of mine, and shall show it unto you.

www.ingramcontent.com/pod-product-compliance
Lightning Source LLC
Chambersburg PA
CBHW031321280626
47169CB00019B/2567